visit us at www.abdopublishing.com

Reinforced library bound edition published in 2012 by Spotlight, a division of the ABDO Group, 8000 West 78th Street, Edina, Minnesota 55439. Spotlight produces high-quality reinforced library bound editions for schools and libraries. Published by agreement with Warner Bros.—A Time Warner Company. The stories, characters, and incidents mentioned are entirely fictional. All rights reserved. Used under authorization.

Printed in the United States of America, Melrose Park, Illinois.
052011
092011
♲ This book contains at least 10% recycled materials.

**Library of Congress Cataloging-in-Publication Data**

Kupperberg, Paul.
  Scooby-Doo in Scooba Doo! / writer, Paul Kupperberg ; artist, Fabio Laguna.
  -- Reinforced library bound ed.
   p. cm. --  (Scooby-Doo graphic novels)
  ISBN 978-1-59961-922-4
1.  Graphic novels.  I. Laguna, Fabio, ill. II. Scooby-Doo (Television program)
III. Title. IV. Title: Scooba Doo.
  PZ7.7.K87Sc 2011
  741.5'973--dc22
                                                2011001370

All Spotlight books are reinforced library bindings
and manufactured in the United States of America.

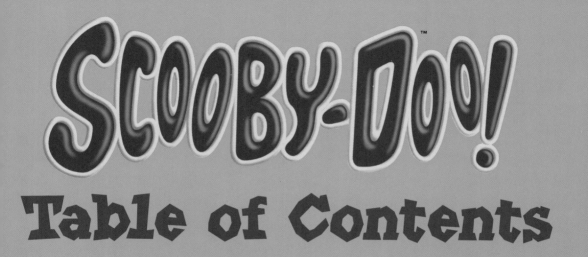

# Table of Contents

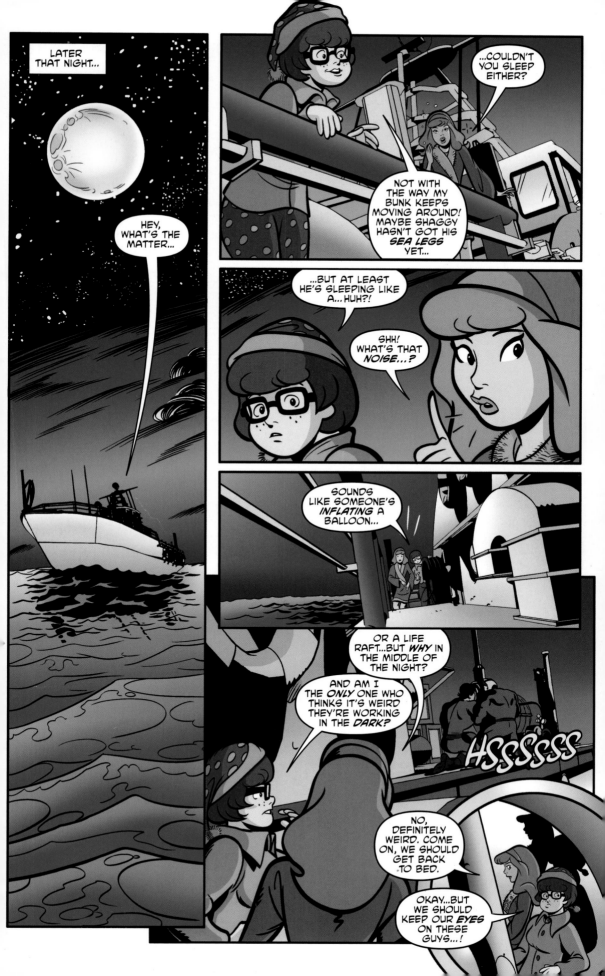

THE NEXT DAY...

ACCORDING TO THE G.P.S., *THIS* WAS THE PRIDE OF SAVANNAH'S POSITION RECORDED BY ELDERBERRY WHEN THE STORM STRUCK...

...SO WE'VE DROPPED ANCHOR AND WE SHOULD BE READY FOR THE FIRST DIVE ANY MINUTE!

ANY SIGN OF THE PRIDE ON YOUR SONAR, CAPTAIN?

HARD TO SAY FOR *SURE*...THE BOTTOM'S PRETTY *ROCKY* OUT HERE.

WE'LL KNOW BETTER ONCE THE DIVERS GET DOWN THERE.

HI, CAPTAIN! THANKS AGAIN FOR LETTING *DAPHNE* AND I DIVE WITH THE GUYS!

I'VE NEVER SEARCHED FOR SUNKEN TREASURE BEFORE!

ER, CAPTAIN GINSBURG...

...ARE YOU *SURE* WE SHOULD BE LETTING THESE KIDS DIVE? WE DON'T KNOW *WHAT'S* DOWN THERE, OR--

THERE'S NO NEED TO *WORRY*, ALVIN.

YOU BET! WE'RE BOTH *QUALIFIED* SCUBA DIVERS!

OH, TYPICAL!

LOST YOUR GLASSES? WE'LL HELP YOU FIND THEM, VELMA!

... AND HERE YOU CAN SEE... A TYPICAL MARK OF...

‡EHHRM...‡ LIKE, DID WE LOSE THE OTHERS? I C-CANT SEE THEM...

THEY CAN'T BE FAR OFF... LET'S WALK THIS WAY AND LOOK FOR THEM!

WH... WHAT?! WHERE DID THEY GO NOW?!

HELP! WE'RE ALONE!!!

OH, NO, WE LOST THE TOUR!

WE BETTER TRY TO FIND THEM...

...OKAY, GIRLS. LEFT OR RIGHT?

RAAAHHH!!

HOW *DARE* YOU WAKE MY ETERNAL SLEEP?! I, MOMAMAZAHH, WILL HAVE MY REVENGE ON *YOU!* YOU WILL NEVER LEAVE THIS CRYPT!

NOW, *THAT* WAS REALLY WEIRD!

I AGREE!

WELL, I FEEL A BIT SPOOKED! WHO KNOWS HOW THESE MUMMY CURSES WORK?!

I'M LIKE, BEGINNING TO THINK WALKING AWAY FROM THE GROUP WASN'T THE BEST IDEA WE'VE EVER HAD, SCOOB!

RAAAAAHHH?

*ZOINKS!* WHAT WAS THAT?! PLEASE TELL ME IT WAS YOUR BELLY!

RO!

TYPICAL! AND WE HAVE NO CLUE HOW TO GET OUT OF HERE! WE DON'T EVEN KNOW WHICH WAY IS *AWAY* FROM THE SCARY NOISE!

WE'LL GO THIS WAY, SCOOB. I DON'T KNOW WHY BUT, LIKE, WE HAVE TO GO SOMEWHERE, RIGHT? JUST CLOSE YOUR EYES AND WE'LL BE FINE!